Justin's Alligator

by Sandra Widener
illustrated by Greg Valley

Harcourt

Orlando   Boston   Dallas   Chicago   San Diego

Visit *The Learning Site!*

www.harcourtschool.com

Justin knew it was not the best idea to bring back an alligator from vacation. He knew that. Even so, this was a very cute baby alligator.

Justin had seen him at a lake. The alligator had said in a tiny alligator voice, "Please?" Justin didn't want to disappoint him. The alligator was very happy.

The first problem was Justin's bag. It was a little small. He had to forcibly stuff the alligator inside. Justin's little sister, June, stared at him and sucked her thumb. Then she said, "Won't he miss the ocean?"

4

Justin's sister was too little to know.
Alligators don't live in oceans.

"No," Justin said very quietly. "He won't
miss it. This is our secret, okay?"

She nodded. Then she said, "What's his name?" Justin didn't know, so he asked. The alligator said, "Honey."

At home, the alligator fit right in. That is, he fit right in, away from Justin's mother. Justin thought his mother would not like a pet alligator.

Justin was a good friend to Honey. Justin found information about what Honey ate— fish, frogs, snakes, and many other things, too. Justin did not need any more details. Dinner scraps would be fine.

Justin's sister found clothes for Honey.
Honey said, "Justin, I will not wear a skirt."

Justin begged, "Please wear it for a while.
You don't want to disappoint my sister."

So Honey wore the skirt. It made him feel
silly, though.

Justin read aloud to Honey and would stroke his back. Then, Honey's tail would spring up. He would also hum. Sometimes the hum was so loud that Justin told him to be quiet.

Honey was learning about all kinds of foods. He told Justin politely that he did like dinner scraps. But he said he liked baked beans, lemon drops, and celery the best.

Honey was a true friend. Trouble was starting, though. Honey ate a lot. Justin had seen his mother looking at him in a funny way. She asked Justin, "When did you start liking celery?"

Also, Honey grew a lot. At first, he fit into a tiny pan. Then he had to be in the bathtub. It was really hard for Justin to keep his mother from seeing Honey.

Justin's mother was studying him all the time. "Since when do you like to take baths so much?" she asked him.

"Since I started eating celery," he said.

Well, it had to happen. One day, Justin's mother went into the bathroom. Honey grinned at her in a friendly way. She let out a yell you could hear for blocks. Soon after that, Honey had to go to the zoo.

Justin was very sad at first. Then Honey told him not to be. Honey liked his new home in the outdoors. He also liked the visits from his best friend, Justin.